Mrs. Union-Wade,

Purposefully Scarred

Thank you for being an inspiration for the black community. Keep shining Queen! Much love,

Kandis Rainey

1

ISBN: 978-1-7352429-6-5

Table of Contents

This book is dedicated to my Granddaddy. William J. Gibbs, Jr I wish I had finished this before you left us. I know that you are in heaven bragging your butt off, saying, "My grandbaby wrote a book!" Thank you for teaching me not to put all my eggs in one basket. I love and miss you so much!

CHAPTER ONE
PURPOSEFULLY SCARRED

I wanted to start by explaining the title of my book: Purposefully Scarred. I plan on talking about this later in the book, but I want to share this part now. After years of fighting the Lord about writing this book, I kind of entertained Him by saying, "If you really want me to write a book, what will the title of it be?"

God speaks to me through my dreams. Just a few nights later, I woke up out of my sleep, grabbed my phone, went to my notes and typed, Purposefully Scarred. The next morning, I remembered what I wrote down. I immediately grabbed my phone and looked up the meaning of the word "purposefully."

Purposefully means in a way that shows determination or resolve and with a useful purpose. I said, "Oh God! You are serious, serious!" What is even crazier is that I looked that up purposefully, like six or seven years ago. I knew what it meant but I had forgotten the actual definition of the word. So, when I did my photoshoot for the cover in August, the way that I have been explaining the meaning of my title and my inspiration for the shoot, just gave me chills.

Anyway, scarred is just what happened to me. In my shoot I wanted to enhance my scar because I wanted people to see the scar and the stitches. Why, you ask? Everything happens for a reason. Good, bad, or indifferent, it is for a reason.

Purposefully Scarred for me, says that the trials you face will sometimes seem to tear you apart. The reality is, before you can heal and grow, you must learn the lessons that God wants you to learn. Like my stiches, the lessons you learn will put you back together.

Use my scar for example, if you look at my scar, every stitch was a lesson. My toughest and most important lessons would be in the middle of my scar. For every lesson I learned, I got a stitch.

I think forgiveness, acceptance, and accountability were my biggest lessons that I needed to learn. Just think, if I did not get three stitches in the middle of my scar, it would have caused a domino effect and caused my entire scar to burst open. "Don't get it yet?"

Sometimes, people go through the same things over and over and never understand why. People always use the phrase, "I take three steps forward and ten steps back." One misstep while climbing a mountain, could cause you to take a few steps back or end up back at the bottom where you started from.

The misstep comes when we do not learn the lessons that He wants us to learn. Until we focus, decide to change, and sacrifice a little bit we will continue to fight the same battles. For example, with some black women, when we don't learn that lesson of forgiveness, we become bitter, angry, resentful, spiteful, or hateful: what some would call a mad black woman. It is sad, but it's true.

Just remember these three things whenever you are facing adversity: 1. God won't put more on us than we can bear. Don't believe it? If you are reading this, you have survived 100% of your toughest days thus far.

2. God will allow you to make the choice to either go left or right. If you go left, do not complain when nothing goes right. If you go right, just know that God is going to make you real uncomfortable and make you go high, when all you wanted to do was go low. God has your back, and he is going to help you weather whatever storm you may face, and you will not look like what you've been through.

3. When adversity strikes, don't "Why me" the Lord to death. No, baby it is "Why not me?" Remember that it happened with purpose intended. You can do anything, just stay the course. You may fall off the course, just don't leave the course. You got this!

CHAPTER TWO
BEFORE THE CUT

Although I did not get cut until 1999, there were several incidents starting in 1997 and continued up until the day that I got cut. The guy involved (let us call him Jrue) and I had what I like to call a "Love & Basketball" relationship.

Every basketball season during high school, we went together and sometimes in the spring/summer as well. Why did we break up so much? He wanted what every high school guy wanted: sex! Personally, I was not going to have sex until I wanted to. When he started having the urge, to have sex, I let him go. Do you, boo.

Ladies, you control your body. Do not allow a man to pressure you to do anything that you don't want to do. It will not make him stay or like you anymore, so you might as well make him wait until you are ready.

The 1997-98 basketball season rolled around and just like any other time we got back together. We both played basketball, so seeing each other daily always brought us back together. I had no idea who he was messing with nor did I care. It was basketball season. We always found our way back to each other.

One day I was walking in the class and the girl involved (let us call her Janae) asked me if she could talk to me. I said yes, but in my mind, I was thinking, "I don't know what the f*** for, but ok." She said, "I just wanted to be woman enough to let you know that your boyfriend has a baby on the way". I responded, "That has nothing to do with me. You need to talk to him about that" and ended the conversation.

Mind you, in 1997 there were hardly any cell phones except the big car cell phones in that big ol' case, so I had to hold it together for a whole 90 minutes just to ask him about Janae being pregnant by him. It gave me time to think and calm down.

In my mind, I felt like the only reason that she came and told me was to get me to break up with him. That was not going to happen now because that's what she wanted me to do.

Ladies stop approaching other women. You are a woman too. Think about it. If another woman approaches you about another man, nine times out of ten, you are not going to stop talking to him just for the hell of it now. Even if you are about to break up with him, you are going to push that back a little bit longer now, just to be petty if for no other reason.

I was no different. If she would have let me find out on my own, I would have left him alone and told him that I did not have time to deal with any baby mamas. Besides all of that, I felt like she came for me and I did not send for her.

Drama only exists if you feed into it. I have always been the type of girl that refuses to fuss with another girl. I never saw the point in it. Girl beef usually stems from the same things: a boy. "You think you're cute", "You think you're better than everybody," "You act stuck up" "I can't stand you." Listen, I am not about to fuss with anybody because you can't stand me. That is a personal problem, Sis! You think you are cute?

I'm confused ladies. Aren't we supposed to be confident in ourselves and think that we are the beautiful women that we are? Y'all, will dislike a chick real quick because she thinks she is cute. Or is the real problem that you know that she is cute?? I act stuck up or think

I'm better than everyone? Clearly, you don't know me.

Just because I don't rock with you doesn't make me stuck up. I probably just caught a bad vibe from you. Everybody ain't supposed to be in your circle or be your cup of tea. That does not mean that I don't like you or that I'm stuck up. I just don't rock with you. That's a big difference.

None of these reasons would ever make me get out of character. I'm like T.I., 'A n*gga put his hands on me alright/ Otherwise stand there, talk sh*t all night' Fussing or fighting over a guy, Why? If he wants you, that's where he should be. There are way too many fish in the sea for that baby girl. Move on to the next guy.

The girl that cut me and I had never gotten into an argument. We fought, but never argued. So, why did we fight? From 1997-1999, Janae fucked with me.

The first year, she was pregnant, even if I wanted to fight her, I couldn't. On top of that, I was an athlete. Nothing was going to stop me from playing sports. Back then, if you got suspended, your season was over with no questions asked. You learned to pick your battles very carefully.

I was called several bitches, I was followed, she acted like she was going to hit my brother's car, and she rode by my house with a car full of people. I lived in a neighborhood that if you didn't live out there, you thought it was one way in and one way out. If you came in my neighborhood, you were looking for someone or visiting someone, period. This crap went on for two years. Jrue and I broke up and got back together and everything during this time.

After the baby was born, I always encouraged him to have a relationship with his daughter and to be more involved in the beginning. I helped pick out Christmas gifts, and if the baby was at the house, I played with her, got her to stop crying, and put her to sleep.

You will understand why I'm telling you this in the next chapter. I'm telling you all of this because although I encouraged the relationship from the beginning and was nice to the little girl, the mother still couldn't stand me.

All women aren't grimy. Oh, there are a lot of grimy women out there, but some women are literally trying to make him a better man. Take the time to see who she really is before you just assume that she is every type of bad woman that you can think of. Just keep in mind everything that I just told you. It's about to go down!

CHAPTER THREE
SHIT JUST GOT REAL

Friday, October 15th, 1999, was the first homecoming after graduating from high school. I turned 18 on September 23rd and I got a 2000 Mercury Cougar (5 speed) for my birthday. I was crazy. I went from a Montero Sport to a two-door cougar. Life was good.

That morning, I was getting some deep wave microbraids and I had a new pair of Nike Air Max Plus that had just dropped. Man, you couldn't tell me nothing. I couldn't wait to go to the homecoming game so I could walk around looking cute.

To be honest, the entire day felt kind of odd. The lady that was braiding my hair was being messy as hell. She scheduled a quick hairstyle when she was supposed to start on my hair. Ugh! So, I had to wait for an hour. I couldn't leave because my hair was a mess and homecoming was that night. When she finally started my hair, she kept stopping.

It was 5 pm. and she still wasn't at the top of my head yet. I had to tell her to do my edges because I had to leave at 7:00 p.m. and I would come back and get it finished. I was lying. My sister was going to finish my hair.

I left shortly after 7:00 p.m. I rushed home, showered, and got dressed. I had not eaten all day, but I was already running late so the concession stand would have to do. I headed straight for the concession stand when

I got to the game, but all I got was some skittles.

As I was turning to leave the concession stand, Jrue's daughter was being held by Janae's friend. Of course, I spoke to the baby. As I was speaking to her, she reached for me to hold her. Her mother was talking to someone to the right of me with her back turned.

When the baby reached for me, the friend and I made eye contact wondering what the hell we should do. We both knew that it was a bad idea for me to hold the baby, but at the same time the baby was reaching for me. Neither one of us knew what to do so, I took the baby, and I held her. I only had her for about 30 seconds before Janae saw it and came to get her.

As she was getting her daughter from me, she turned to her friend and said, "You know I have to go and get my baby (she was talking about Jrue)." I heard it but I didn't pay it any mind but that was shots fired. My friends and I went to the concession stand during halftime.

Although I was hungry, I still didn't get anything to eat. Before returning to the stands for the second half, I left without telling anybody that I was leaving, which was very odd. By the time I got in my car, I was starving, but I didn't know what I wanted to eat. I changed my mind three times in a matter of two minutes.

I was getting close to Captain D's and something says, "Go to Captain D's", which was very odd since I rarely eat there. There are five lanes and I'm going east. I was in the left lane and Captain D's was on the right, so I had to cut across a lane and turn right away or I would miss my turn. Of course, there would be no cars stopping me from cutting across and making the turn.

I never saw Janae's car until I turned into the parking lot of Captain D's. I looked up and I see Jrue sitting in the passenger seat. I felt like I was in a movie, and we were moving in slow motion. They looked at me and I looked at them as we rode past each other.

It was the longest, shortest stare down ever. I was thinking, "Ohhhhhhhhh, that's the baby she had to pick up." Noted! Here's the funny part. I'm driving a 5-speed, but I still haven't mastered it yet. Trying to get out of first gear was a struggle.

I cut off about three times while I was trying to turn around to follow them. If you would have seen me jerking in that car you would've died laughing. You're probably rolling on the floor right now.

I never prayed so hard for green lights before in my life because I did not want to have to stop. My prayers worked. I finally get behind them about a mile away from Captain D's and they pull over in a vacant parking lot.

Listennnnnnnnnnn, I promise on everything, I had no intentions on saying a word to her, let alone fight her. I didn't have a problem with her for having him in the car. It was his ass that I had a damn problem with because he shouldn't have been in the car with her if he was my boyfriend.

My plan was for Janae to let him out, leave, and then I would leave him stranded in the parking lot. He didn't have a cell phone so he would have had to walk and find a payphone. To be honest, it was a horrible plan.

Who plans like that and they can't get out of first gear? I would have stalled out and he would have caught me. The way the parking lot was set up it wasn't a straight shot so it would have been really hard to get away from him. It would have been an epic failure.

When she stopped the car, he got out of the car and we started arguing. I see her chilling in the car with her window down, listening. She was messing up my damn plan. So, I said to her, "You can leave now." And she said, "I'll wait for him to tell me to leave."

Listennnnnn, I'm trying my hardest not to snap on her, but she is really trying me. I just rolled my eyes and kept fussing with him. At some point, he said, "Let me tell her to leave." As he turned to tell her to leave, I had a quick flashback of all of the shit that she had done and said with the last thing being, 'I'll wait for him to tell me to leave' with a smirk on her face.

Most of our encounters happened on campus, this was the first time we weren't on a campus. Except for her riding through my neighborhood but she wouldn't even stop then. I think she thought I was scared of her because I never addressed her. Nope, I always had something to lose and none of the stuff she said or did bothered me. And she came for me once again and I didn't send for her.

When you've never been in a real fight, deep down, you are nervous about fighting because you really don't know how good you are at it. I was a three-sport athlete and a gymnast so, my physical strength was never a question, it was the fighting part that made me nervous.

I felt this unexplainable feeling takeover my body and I completely blacked out. As he was walking to the car, I pushed him out of the way and punched her in the face while she was sitting in the car. After I landed that first punch, I knew I would be fine fighting.

He pushed me away from her car and asked me, "Why did I do that?" I was looking over his shoulder the whole time watching her. I simply said, "It doesn't even matter now. Get out of the way." He moved out of the way.

As he moved away, I saw her cut the light on in her car and look around for something. My adrenaline was pumping, I never thought about what she could have been looking for. I never thought she would intentionally do something to hurt me, but I was about to find out otherwise.

As she was walking over to me, I heard something clicking but it honestly sounded like a lighter. If it was a lighter, I was thinking there is no way you can fight and strike a lighter at the same time. So, we started fighting and I forgot all about whatever she had in her hand.

This was my first fight, so after about 35 seconds into the fight, which seemed like two minutes, I felt blood all over the side of my face, but she hadn't hit me in my face though. So, I'm like WTF? We fought for what seemed like another two minutes but was probably 45 seconds to a minute later and I started feeling weak as hell.

I weighed 135 pounds, I hadn't eaten all day, and blood was gushing out of my face. Ohhhhhh, I'm about to get my ass beat. I remember being on one knee and her punching me on my head and I was thinking, "you better think of something fast."

I know you guys are wondering, where in the hell was Jrue? He was lighting a black and mild. Yep, I remember seeing that during the fight. All I could think to say was, "I don't even know why we are fighting!" That was the dumbest thing ever. I hit her first, of course I knew why we were fighting.

I think I meant to say, "I don't even know why you don't like me." She paused and said, "I don't know either." When she paused, my braids were covering my face, so I pushed them back. Me pushing my braids back saved me because now they both could see what she had done.

As I was getting up, he said, "Look what you did to her face!" and he slapped her. I said, "Boy, what are you thinking? It's just a bunch of blood." He said, "Duhhhh, but where is it coming from Kandis?" She jumped into her car and left. I thought to myself, Oh, so now you wanna leave?

My mind went right back to my original plan which was to leave him stranded in the parking lot. I hurried to my car. Before I could close my door, he grabbed the door saying, "We need to get you to the hospital." I heard him say hospital, but I didn't hear it. My adrenaline was pumping. I said, "I'm not going to the hospital. I'm going home."

I pushed him out of the way so I could close my door. Something said Kan, "You really should look in the mirror." I pulled my visor down and opened that mirror and I saw that scar. I just fell out of my car onto the ground crying. It had started raining, but I didn't even care. I couldn't believe what just happened to me.

He picked me up and put me in the passenger side of the car and drove me to the hospital. On the way to the hospital, I realized that my ring fingernail had been ripped completely off and I had blood on my sneakers. Instead of focusing on the scar, I focused on the blood on my sneakers.

Sneakerheads don't play about stuff like that. It brought me down 100 notches, which is what I needed. My boyfriend called my mom and told her what happened and that he was taking me to the hospital. I have bigger problems now. How is my family going to react to this? Lord, send help!

I arrived at the hospital and talked to the police. After they left, I was alone. Everything hit me at once and I just started balling. I'm talking about ugly face cry with a pause in it type of cry. God knew exactly what I needed and exactly when I needed it. He sent help. He sent the most amazingly calm nurse into my room. Well, it wasn't a room. It was an area separated by curtains.

When she walked in, my mom and sister had to be walking in the emergency room because she gave me some tissue and said, "You need to calm down because your family doesn't need to see you like this." Boy was she right! If she hadn't reminded me of that, the rest of this story would be totally different.

As soon as she said it, I heard the hospital doors burst open like A-Wax did after Caine got shot in Menace II Society: hard and loud! When they ripped the curtain open, I was as cool as the outside of the pillow. The bandage freaked my mom out and she had a moment.

It was much better than it could have been. A couple of weeks prior to my incident, my local hospital did a botch job on somebody's arm. I was advised by a nurse that my initial stitches needed to be done correctly. To Virginia, I go. Virginia hospitals reputation were better than our local hospital.

While waiting to be discharged, they were trying to bandage my face, I said, "That can wait! Can you please do something about my finger?" My finger felt as if it was hanging off and I needed something for the pain. I asked for Morphine and they totally ignored me.

After they released me, my boyfriend had a genuinely sincere moment outside with my mom, sister, his mom, and me. He cried as he apologized for his part and said that he never meant for any of this to happen.

That was the first time I'd ever seen him cry. I noticed a change in him right after it happened so, seeing tears didn't surprise me at all. That talk and tears made this ride that we were about to take possible. I knew my mom and sister weren't as mad at him. They knew I wasn't fighting for no reason and over him either.

I drove up to a hospital in Virginia with my mom, sister, her boyfriend, and Jrue which was about 45 mins away to get my face stitched up. As I'm riding to the hospital, I realized that this was no longer just about me. Now, I had to worry about my mom, sister, and my brother's reaction to all of this.

Knowing the people in my family the way that I do, it was going to go something like this. My mom is a Momma Bear, especially in this situation because I literally don't mess with anyone. So, she was going to lose it when she heard about it and wanted to bring havoc to everyone associated with her---mom, dad, sister, brother, cousin, dog, employer, or friends. Nobody was exempt. Anybody could get it.

My sister will only throw hands when necessary and she is like seven years older than Janae, and that's a kid to her. Real talk, when she cut me, fighting was out of the question for her. She actually said, "There's no need for both of us to get cut but there are some other ways to get her."

You have to know when my sister wants something to happen, it's going to happen by any means necessary. When I say she can have the President of any company on the phone by 10 am to report your ass, that's exactly what the hell I mean. She is a whole other type of gangster.

My brother on the other hand is the big brother of all big brothers. If I call, no matter how big or small it is, he is coming. No questions asked. Since I know how he is, if there's the slightest chance that he can get in any type of trouble, I'm not calling him. It will always mean more to me to be able to call, talk, and/or see my brother whenever I want to. Yeah, he's not going down for no dumb shit.

I can handle myself. In tough situations, you have to figure out who needs you more or who you need more. In my situation, I needed my family more. I didn't need anyone in jail or going to court behind my mistakes. So, I needed to smooth things over by any means necessary.

When we arrived at the hospital in Virginia, my brother was pacing around outside. We didn't even know that he knew what had happened to me, but he beat us there. I thought, "Oh, shit! What's his reaction going to be because Jrue is here."

I started sweating nervously. I knew that the most important thing to him was to make sure that his baby sister was okay, but I also knew that the big brother in him wanted to beat Jrue's ass and there was no way that I could let that happen, but I'll get to this a little later.

I jokingly asked my brother did he take a jet to get to the hospital because there is no way that he drove there that fast. It was my brother. He absolutely drove that fast. As we waited in the emergency room, there was a level of awkwardness and tension in the air that you could only imagine.

I went to the bathroom while we were waiting, I looked in the mirror and tears rolled down my face. I realized that my bigger task was going to be keeping my family calm on top of dealing with everything that came along with having this scar: known and unknown.

The pressure on my shoulders felt like boulders. I dropped my head and looked back in the mirror. If Issa Rae was popping back then, I probably would have busted a rap to myself to get me together. My reflection said, "You can keep crying and feel sorry for yourself or suck it up and keep it moving because either way, it's still going to be there."

I wiped my face and never cried about it again. With the tension in the waiting room, I had bigger fish to fry. I had no time for tears. This situation was no longer just about me.

I knew that when they called me back only two people could go back with me. My mom and sister were definitely going back. In the waiting room, that left my brother, Jrue, and my sister's boyfriend.

My sister's boyfriend was very helpful in this situation. He was an instant comic relief and a great middleman, and most importantly, he kept my sister calm. I knew that when we went in the back, he would keep my brother calm, and talk some real shit to Jrue as well. Just from a standpoint of what everyone was feeling and how he had to understand and respect everyone's feelings, how everyone was going to look at him, and how he needed to prepare himself for any backlash.

52 stitches later (49 in the face and 3 under my arm), I was headed home. It was Saturday morning, by the time we got home. I slept half of the next day to avoid talking to a bunch of nosey ass people. I could tell by the conversations that my sister was having that I needed a plan.

CHAPTER FOUR
THINKING OF A MASTER PLAN

I realized that I needed a plan. I needed to know how I wanted to handle my family, my friends, haters, and people in the community. I had to think about how much I wanted people to know, and how I wanted everyone to view me. I wanted to be prepared for as much as possible.

I had court Monday morning, a 3:00 pm class, and volleyball practice at 6:00 pm. All of which I planned to attend. I had to come up with a plan ASAP.

I realized, if I was awake there were nonstop conversations with family or their friends calling trying find out what happened. So, when I needed to think, I pretended to be asleep. Sleeping has always been one of my favorite things to do so it wouldn't look out of the ordinary for me to sleep a lot.

I'm from a very small town, where everyone knew everybody, and everyone knew about what had happened to me by now. The great thing is that we didn't have a ton of cell phones or social media during this time. There were only landlines and pagers.

What in the world was I going to say and do? How was I going to get through this? This is the plan that I came up with: I had to draw my own conclusion about why she cut me so I could have closure.

I figured she did this to try and make me look less attractive, to hurt me, my reputation, and to make me break up with him. I know you are all thinking, breaking up with him should have been a given, but for me, everything had changed. Yeah, I know you think I'm the biggest dummy ever. It's cool. Staying with him protected him and he was my protection.

My plan was to do the opposite of what everybody thought I would do. I was going to have a smile on my face, stay with my boyfriend, stay out and about, share what I wanted to share with people, and not let this scar define me.

I found that having a plan made dealing with people easier. I knew what I wanted to say and what I wouldn't discuss at all. Knowing how I wanted to handle things allowed me to stay focused and not get sucked into all the chatter and bullshit. When going through an ordeal that everyone knows about, it's important to stick to your guns. Stick to your values and do what you feel is best for you.

CHAPTER FIVE
ACCEPTANCE, ACCOUNTABILITY, &
FORGIVENESS

Acceptance

Acceptance is something that I felt was necessary for me to attempt to forgive her. In my situation, I had to accept the fact that I would probably have this scar on my face the rest of my life and it would forever be a part of me.

I had to accept the fact that no matter how much I cried about it, it would still be there. No matter how many times I retaliated, it would still be there. Accept the fact that if I wanted to even the score, my scar would still be there.

Accept that no matter how mad it made me; it would still be there. If I hid from the world, it would still be there. If I decided to feel sorry for myself, it would still be there. On the days where my scar looked the size of my face and I would rather stay home but I had to go out, it was still there.

I had to accept the fact that some people would assume that I was this woman who was mean and liked to fight all the time. I had to accept the fact that the Kandis I was before October 15th,1999, had changed forever. I had to accept the fact that however I handled the situation, would determine how my family handled the situation.

I had to accept the fact that people wanted to see me fail. I had to accept that I may never know why this happened or get an apology and be okay with it. Once I accepted the situation for what it was, my thought process changed. Once that happened, it was a wrap! Accepting the situation for what it was made the comeback easy. I accepted it, so what now? Oh, it's time to slay bitch!

In my mind, more people wanted me to fail or for the scar to ruin me than those who wanted me to bounce back. With that being said, I was determined to show everyone that this scar wouldn't break me, nor would it define me.

I was determined to make my smile and my eyes outshine the scar that was on my face. Learn to accept the obstacles in front of you and tap into the G.O.A.T. that lives inside of you! Michael Jordan is the G.O.A.T because of all the hard work that he put in to perfect his craft but also because of that "can't nobody stop me" type of attitude.

When Beyonce steps on stage as Sasha Fierce, she knows that she's about to shut the internet down again. Just because we aren't famous doesn't mean that we can't have that same attitude in our everyday life.

If you know like I do, you better, because there's someone out there waiting for you to fall flat on your face. Don't give them the satisfaction. Dig deeper than ever and get up every time life knocks you down and ask who or what's next?

Accountability

Accountability is the part that most people like to overlook. I held myself accountable to the fact that I hit her first. Since I knew that I started the fight, I needed to apologize. I knew that deciding to apologize to her first would cause a whole lot of chaos. I knew that everyone would disagree with my decision, and they still do. That's why I chose not to tell a soul.

I did what was best for ME. I did what would allow me to sleep peacefully at night. Nobody that would have advised me to not apologize would have lost sleep. Remember to always do what's best for you and not worry about what people are going to say about your decisions. It's YOUR life. Do what's best for YOUR life! "The true test of a man's character is what he does when no one is watching. -- John Wooden.

When I teach, I like to hold my students accountable. They never seem to understand why or where they went wrong in the situation. That's where I come in. Yep, I break it all the way down and I make them stand in the other person's shoes so that they can see just how it feels to have it done to them. Then, we talk about better ways to handle the situation the next time.

Although most of the time when we have those talks in middle school or high school, they don't get it at the moment. I have had many kids thank me later. It's crazy because I tell them that they probably won't understand what I was saying at the time but one day the light bulb will go off and they will remember what Coach Riddick/Rainey said. To all the students that have thanked me, the migraine that you gave me trying to explain that to you was all worth it! I love y'all, and I mean it!

Sometimes you just don't see where you are wrong. That's why it's important to have people in your corner that will hold you accountable and not just be your yes-man. You know what a yes-man is. That person that will just go along with all your madness and never check your ass when you are dead wrong. They aren't your friend. If you knew better, you would do better!

Real friends will check your ass and you will respect them because you know that they are keeping it real. Now, don't get them confused with the friends that will check you but when they do the exact same thing, that same advice that they gave you, doesn't apply to them. They aren't your real friend either. They secretly want you to fail. Watch their ass for real.

On a serious note, hold yourself accountable and surround yourself with people that will do the same. Don't be afraid to apologize when you should. Especially after you've had time to assess the whole situation and understand all sides involved. Be real about it.

If you overreacted, jumped to a conclusion, assumed, made an ass of yourself, or just fucked up, apologize. Apologize with the intent of clearing the air with a sincere heart, whether they accept it or not. The ball is now in their court.

Now, some of you need to understand that ONE apology doesn't mean that everything is forgiven. Nahhh player, you don't get to decide how much you hurt someone or when they should be over it! If they need time, give them time. Don't rush them, Be patient. Hold yourself and others accountable. That allows you and the people around you to grow on another level.

Forgiveness

Forgiveness is everything and more importantly, it's for you! "Strength is forgiving people that don't even feel sorry for their actions" Strength is also forgiving people and never knowing the real reason why. In either case, forgive them anyway!

When you refuse to forgive someone, you give them power over you. You don't believe me? Let somebody that has wronged you, walk into the room right now. I bet you money that your whole entire mood will change. You will become hot as fish grease, and you know that's hot! They have power over you. The crazy part is they know it.

They will literally cross paths with you on purpose because they know it will set you off. Yeah, that ex of yours is fucking with you. They know that it pisses you off seeing them. You have to turn the tables and forgive them. So, the next time that they bring their ass around, you can speak to them and wish them well. Now, who's mad now? Not you!!

One of the best feelings in the world is seeing that one person that manages to press every last one of your buttons and even finds buttons that you didn't even know that you had, and they no longer piss you completely off.

You can go high with a smile, while they are still trying to go low with a frown.

The glow hits different when you let go and let God deal with it. When you can wish them the best, no stress, success, and lots of happiness and mean it. Finally getting that monkey off your back is the best feeling ever! Now, that's growth!

See, here's the thing people (in my Kevin Hart voice) you should learn to forgive people no matter how bad they hurt you. Forgiveness turns into a ton of weight off your shoulders. I remember the first time that I apologized was within the first week of it happening. Although I meant it, I personally hadn't truly forgiven her yet. I realized that I still had a little animosity in my heart.

I could tell because for a couple of months, if someone asked me what happened or who did it, I would say her name and that she cut me in the face. I remember one day saying that and heard a little voice say, "Do you feel better now? Now, look in the mirror. It's still there Kan! You must stop saying that shit. There's no point!"

That little voice inside of me was right but man, I just wanted to be petty. Before I went to bed that night, I prayed for the Lord to take her name out of my mouth and not let it roll off of my tongue again and asked to help me forgive her wholeheartedly.

The next day, I felt some weight lifted off my shoulders. After that, I decided that I would speak to Janae every time that I saw her. When I would ride past her, I would throw my hand up to speak. I never even looked to see what her reaction to it was. I didn't care nor did it matter. She could've given me the finger for all I know but it didn't matter.

I remember one time I had my friend in the car and the girl rode past me and I spoke. My friend said, "Why in the hell are you speaking to her?" My reply to her was, "Why in the hell not? I'm not mad at her anymore." I also explained to her that if the girl called me a bitch, talked shit about me, or even told the story to anyone, they would look at her and say, "If she's not mad at you and you cut her, why in

62

the hell are you mad at her." Things that make you say, hmmmmm!

Until this day, it's rare if I say who cut me. IF I tell my students what happened, I never tell them who did it. It doesn't matter, I just need for them to learn from my mistakes. Forgiveness is one of those things in life that if you don't learn to do it, it will ruin your life. It will keep you in this dark ass place in life.

Holding onto all that pain turns you into this bitter, angry, nasty, vindictive, spiteful, resentful, raging, depressed, sad person. It also makes you unattractive on the inside and out, stressed out, and so many more things. All those things will lead to mental, physical, health, and social problems.

Yes, the traumatic events that take place can cause those issues as well but by prolonging those issues, and by not forgiving them is on you! Take my situation, I could have let my feelings and everybody's else shoulda, woulda, couldas turn into rage. All that rage would have made me bitter. The bitter and rage would have had me retaliate, leaving me with serious charges that would have made being successful a struggle with felony charges. The charges would have turned me into a bitter and resentful person.

Now, I really would have been the angry girl with the scar on her face. All that would have done would have wasted my time and my life. Remember nobody says that you should forget what they did, like them, or try to be

BFFs with them. Just forgive them so that they don't have control over you.

You only get one life. Do whatever you need to do to help you make peace with yourself, the situation, and the people that love you. Forgive them, let go, and let God deal with the rest.

CHAPTER SIX
PUBLIC PROBLEM

After receiving my scar, I honestly realized how celebrities felt when going through anything on a much smaller scale of course. When you have a public problem, all eyes are on you. People that normally wouldn't pay you, any attention, are now focused on you.

I'm talking about old people, young people, white people, church people, Chinese people, people that don't know you, it doesn't matter. Everyone is looking at you. Everyone is looking to see how you're going to handle the situation. Are you going to rise or fall?

Girls were praying that I would fall off. I was fortunate enough that my incident took place before the cell phone, social media, and screenshot era. It was much easier to control the narrative without the three. Some of the stories that I've heard of what happened to me have been absolutely insane.

Public problems become the topic of discussion everywhere. Everyone is trying to be the first one to report the news. Everyone is trying to call you or find people closest to you to find out what happened.

Know that only about twenty percent of the people that you hear from care about how you are doing. The other eighty percent just want to know what happened so they can go back and tell people. Be clear, that goes for everyone: family, friends, cousins, coworkers, church people, etc. Nobody is exempt.

Watch how quick they get to "So, what really happened?" That's all they really care about anyway. The great thing about me is I never really fooled with a lot of people, so very few people had access to me. So, I didn't receive a lot of random calls.

People are always going to add to, take away, and stretch the truth, so it's really important what you share with other people about your situation. They want you to say any little thing about the other person so they can stretch the truth to keep shit going. Not that you don't already have enough real shit going on, now you have to worry about shit that you didn't say.

People just want to be the first to say, well I got it from the horse's mouth and still lie! Once all the stories and lies have been told, now you are really under a microscope whenever you go out. Everybody is watching me to see just how the "pretty girl" will handle the scar on her face. Knowing in the back of my mind half of them wanted it to mess my life and my appearance up.

Cardi B wasn't even out in 1999 but I already had her mindset, "I'm steppin' out every day, prom night." All that means is when I stepped out of the house, I would be all the way together. Literally, that was my mindset.

My major was Physical Education, so it was nothing for me to go to a gym class bummy. Not after this, when I wore athletic clothing, I matched from head to toe Everything had to be just so and neatly placed. I've always presented well but after this I couldn't have a hair out of place. Normal people keep their braids a couple of months. Not me. I had to get them touched up halfway through.

I had to smile or have a pleasant look on my face while out and about. If not, Kandis never has a smile on her face or I haven't seen Kandis in forever. Lord forbid, If I had a bad hair day or bummy day (which was the norm), the people would be saying, "Oh lawd Lord, have you seen Kandis today? She is going through. Her hair is a mess, and I don't know what in the hell she had on. This situation is about to take her out."

It's crazy because I could have been sick, had family problems, my face could have been hurting, just one of them days or anything but people would just assume the scar was the reason for my mood. All the staring was a little tough at first. I learned quickly that if everyone could sense that it was uncomfortable for me, they would continue to stare and make being around me awkward.

I had to learn to become comfortable with it, so the people around me would too. I wanted my smile and sense of humor to lighten the mood. I learned to literally laugh through my pain until my public problem was no longer a problem.

Remember when you are going through a public problem, in order to control the public, you have to control your mouth. The more you talk, the more times your story will get told and turned around. You and your problems will stay relevant.

Stop talking about it and something else will happen to take their mind off you and your problems. If you have done something bad, own up to your shit and leave it at that. If you own your shit, it will go away faster than you think. The people do not know how to respond to that, so they just shut up.

CHAPTER SEVEN
WHAT ABOUT YOUR FRIENDS?

I have always been that "Ride or Die Friend." You got beef, we got beef! Point. Blank. Period! I was never super close to many but the ones that I was close with, I had their back. Even after being cut, my friends did not know that I looked at them differently, but I did. They knew that Kan had their back. I still do, just not like before.

After the incident, God said, "I want you to pay attention to everybody's reaction. Pay attention to who will fight for you and who really has your back, and I want you to act accordingly." I did just that! This situation was such an eye opener for me.

I had to be the most gullible and naive 18-year-old around before this happened. I managed to still have love for my friends and people, but it just changed how I looked and dealt with them, especially females. With my female friends, I handled them differently because this one conversation made the light bulb go off. This is what happened.

Shortly after the incident, I ran into Janae's best friend at her job. She said, "I heard that you and some of your friends are planning to jump my girl! She is like my sister, so I'm not having that!" I was under the influence at the time, so what she said never registered until I came down. So, when I addressed her, I was super calm.

To be honest, the friend that I was, I would have said the said damn thing whether they were wrong or right. I would not have said anything, I would have just fought them for cutting one of my friends. When she said that, I was thinking, "Who in the hell have you been talking to because none of my friends were talking about jumping no damn body. Hell, they did not even utter the word fight, jump, or retaliate. That is when the light bulb went off.

Why was Janae's friend down to ride for her and she cut me? Why aren't any of your friends riding for you? From that moment on, I changed. I became really guarded and to myself. Until this day, I do not mind rolling alone and most of the time I prefer it. I realized that my beef was my beef, and their beef was theirs. If you call me, I am coming but just to make sure that it's fair game.

From that moment to the present, I am only fighting for those who will go to blows for me. If you don't understand that, we aren't meant to be friends. Once people show you where you stand, believe them. Now, I will always make sure that it is one on one. If they were getting beat up, my job would be to stop it. You get your friend, and I will get mine.

I remember somebody getting jumped in the city and we were all talking about it. I told everybody that was there, "I'm not asking any of you to fight for me but if I get jumped and you don't want to fight, just break it up because if I find out that any of you were there and did nothing, I'm coming to your house and going to beat your ass. I am not listening to no, "see what had happened was." I meant that with everything in me.

I knew some of them were not going to fight for me, so I was giving them a heads up. The lesson that I needed to learn from this, is that I can expect ME from other people. This is something that I still struggle with to this very day. I cannot expect others to respond the same way that I would. By doing that, I am just setting myself up to be disappointed.

When I expect me from someone else and I do not receive that at times, it makes me question the individual's intentions at times. I have to remind myself that everyone is not going to respond the way that you would and makes me take the time to see where they are coming from. It does not make them a bad person or a bad friend, they just handle things differently than me.

All our friends are different. You know who the fighter is, the shit talking one, the bougie one, the scared one, the quiet one, the turnt up one, etc. you know who everyone in your crew is. This situation just opened my eyes to that, and it was just what I needed at 18.

The sooner you learn who your friends really are, how they react, and handle things you will know exactly what to expect from them. The crazy part is that as I am was writing this, I realized that for almost two years after the fight, I rarely kicked it with anyone other Jrue, his brother, and his best friend.

I hung out between classes but other than that, I did not see them. This is why I stayed with him; he had my back! Slapping her was wrong as hell, but he did that because of what she did to me. After that, we did everything together. When I say everything, I mean everything.

We cooked, washed the car, played pick up ball, took naps, chilled, laughed, cried, joked, and went to church. You name it, we did it, together. I knew that he had my back no matter what the situation was. At that moment, that meant everything to me.

CHAPTER EIGHT
THE EXPERTS OF NOTHING
(LAUGHABLE BULLSHIT)

When you are going through an ordeal, it is very important that you try and make decisions when your mind is the clearest. Most importantly, always do what is best for you and the people that you love. I keep saying that because it is so important. So, please stay away from laughable bullshit.

One of the things that kept me sane was not listening to the opinions of people who have not been through the shit that I have been through. They have expert advice for you, but they have never been through what you have. How can you give me advice on something you know nothing about? Laughable Bullshit, right?

Of course, everyone can tell you what they would do if they were in your situation, but it is all lies! The truth of that matter is that you never really know what you are going to do in a situation until it happens. For example, when I was in middle school, I remember hearing about someone getting cut in their face. I can remember talking about it at school during lunch with my friends.

Everyone at the table said what they would do if it happened to them. Guess what I said? I said, "if that happened to me, I would put a brown bag over my head." Five or six years later, it actually happened to me! Crazier part is, a few hours after being cut, I had a flashback to that very conversation. That little person in my mind said, "Would you like for me to get you a brown paper bag?" My immediate thought was, "For what?"

I had no intentions of covering my face, hiding in the house, frowning, or turning into the angry black woman that the world would expect me to, or anything close to that. My plans were the complete opposite. My sister being the prissy one that she is, bought me some concealer. Girl bye! I ain't wearing that.

You never know how you are going to react to something until it happens to you. That little middle school Kandis had no idea what she could withstand when thrown in the fire, but she would soon find out. Back to the experts of nothing. I let all the shoulda, woulda, coulda, people entertain me. I listened to all the shit that they would have done, would do, and/or the shit that they would do. First of all, people (in my Kevin Hart voice), look at the person who is talking? Have you ever known them to at least pinch a bitch before? I will wait.

Do not let a person that has never laid a hand on anyone, hype you up to retaliate or make you think that they have your back. They will not have it. You know who is willing to catch a charge and who is not. Those people will ghost you when the situation gets real, reappear when everything calms down, and then say, "I didn't really think that you were going to do it, or you shouldn't have done that!" Really, bih? It was your idea.

Do not let them talk you into having to spend unnecessary money on hospital bills or bail. This is the one thing that I wish the younger generations would learn. Kids these days tend to react and not think about all the people that it affects. It does not matter to them.

If you take a life, it affects that person's entire family: parents, sisters, brothers, kids, aunts, uncles, cousins, friends, nieces, nephews, classmates, coworkers, grandparents, teachers, and community. Not to mention all those same people in your life. You have got to stop just thinking about yourself at that moment.

Everybody keeps saying that they want respect. Respect is earned, young people. Disrespect is also earned. You want respect from people that do not respect their own families. Please, tell me why they are going to respect you? You want respect from people who cannot do nothing for you and disrespect the people that do everything for you. Stop dishing out what you cannot take.

Think about your kids and your families before you do the things that will cause you to end up in jail, the hospital, or worse, dead. I'm tired of seeing R.I.P.'s for nonsense. We are in a whole Pandemic and we still have to worry about senseless violence. This is a conversation for another time. Young people you have got to do better.

It is all laughable bullshit because they don't know what they would do and most importantly, it doesn't mean that it's best for you and your situation. If the people giving you advice are not encouraging, motivating, uplifting, praying for you, or giving you a better perspective, stop talking to them. They are only there for entertainment. Learn to let them entertain you for a bit and then get back to your regularly scheduled program: Your life and what is best for it.

CHAPTER NINE
UNPRETTY MOMENTS PITY PARTIES

This is a topic that I really do not like discussing but I feel it's necessary to address. As a female, it is one of those moments that we have all experienced. Feeling unpretty. So much that TLC wrote a whole song about it and why I named this chapter after it.

Every time that I say that I have an "Unpretty moment" regarding this scar, everyone will comment with things like, "You are beautiful regardless" or "Don't let anything make you feel anything less than beautiful." I did not mention it for sympathy, it's just a transparent moment. Listen Sis, I am definitely not the type of woman who doesn't think that she isn't beautiful. I was raised with a crown on my head. I have always been confident enough to compliment another woman on her beauty as well.

I know there will be plenty who will say, "Who does she think she is?" Me: A very confident woman nine out of ten days. So, where do the unpretty moments come from? The first couple of years after the incident, I had days that all I could see was this scar on my face. In those moments, I struggled. On those days, no makeup, concealer, best hairdo, or outfit could change what I saw at that moment.

My moments are no different than a woman having a pimple, blemishes, bags under her eyes, bloating, birthmark, thinning edges, a bald spot, mole, or whatever else you may struggle with. It is days that my face will break out and that's all I see-no scar either. Other days, my skin will seem flawless to the point that I have to check and see if my scar is still there.

Notice that I said "moment." Ladies, whenever this happens, let it be for just that, a moment. Do not let the unpretty moments turn into days, weeks, months, or even years. When that happens, walk away from the mirror. The longer you look in the mirror, the worst it is going to get. Know that you are beautiful no matter the situation.

If you are dealing with pimples or a mole, think of me, the lady with a scar, and smile because it could be worse. Look at yourself in the mirror and remind yourself of who you really are. If that does not work, bust an Issa Rae verse, grab some lip gloss, smile, and walk out of the house with confidence. Remember that you are that chick without saying a word or letting anyone know how real the struggle was on that day.

Real beauty and confidence exude the most on the days that we struggle the most. The days that I have unpretty moments, God will always use someone, and a random person will say, "Good Morning, beautiful!" or "You look awesome today!" It is the subtle reminders for me.

Have you ever had an unpretty moment and looked at a picture that you took later that day and realized how fabulous you looked? Yes, it happens to me all the time. If you have not completely convinced yourself that you are a Badddd Bihhhhhh before you have to face the world turn on that one song that brings your alter ego out. Everybody has that one song, if you do not please go find one right now. Throw a bookmark in this book and find that song that gives your life. Play it on repeat.

After Survivor came out, I can guarantee you that 95% of the time, that song was blasting in my car. I needed everyone that thought I would not last with this shit (scar), that I was lasting! Periodt! Yes, you must convince yourself of some things but if you say or do it enough you will start to believe it.

Pity Party

Everybody goes through their own struggles and that is ok. What is not ok is that you sit around and wallow in your pity. Some of you wallow in your pity so much and so long that it becomes what I like to call this big elaborate pity party. I mean it feels like you hire a party planner and everything. You try to invite everybody and their momma to the party.

The people that will join you at this party are the people that will sit down the whole time or hold up the wall. They are miserable too and know that misery loves company. Listen, everybody is going through something. Ain't nobody got time for that! Yes, your friends will listen and allow you to vent from time to time about your problems, but nobody wants to hear about it every single time that you come around. Ugh! Especially, if you are part of the problem. Then, you are wondering why people do not return your calls or why people are heading for the door as soon as you come around.

People are tired of you and the pity party. Folks have cut the lights on, cleaned up, broke the table and chairs down, took the trash out, and left the building on your ass. The people are tired of hearing about it. We are all struggling with something in one way or another. It is all about how you deal with everything that is thrown your way. If you are really struggling, seek some professional help.

People do not mind helping people that don't mind helping themselves. It is the hardheaded, victim playing ones that tear everybody's nerves up. Stop feeling sorry for yourself or playing the victim. You are stronger than that. Have your moment, pray on it, and move on.

CHAPTER TEN
SURVIVING ON PURPOSE

If you do not get anything else from this book, I want you to get this. Survive on Purpose. Do whatever it is that you need to do to survive, the right way. Be determined to live a better life. Stop complaining and blaming others. Take control of the things that you can control and the things that you cannot control.

Control how you respond and deal with those things. If you need to go to therapy, go! Nobody has to know but you and your therapist. If it makes you feel more comfortable, find a therapist that does not live in your area. A therapist needs a therapist, and you think you do not? We all need one.

I know that the Black Community will have you thinking that you do not need to go to therapy. Boy, you better go get a blunt or a bottle and forget about that shit. The blunt turns into a crack pipe, a needle, or a bottle or two a day. All you are doing is running from your problems. Those problems are following your ass around like the hood on your coat. It is going everywhere that you go.

Some of your families have made you keep that shit to yourself for so long that you think that it is not a problem or affecting your life. It is affecting most of your decisions, the way you act, think, or how you respond to things. Cut toxic people off. If you must deal with toxic people, limit your time with them.

Protect your mental headspace by any means necessary. You cannot let them get the last word or get one over on you. Stop listening! If you do not like hanging up on people, learn to (or at least say that your signal dropped) put the phone down so that you can't even hear what they are saying. If you do not know what they are saying, you can't respond to their madness. If they text you a long message, fussing, do not read it. Especially, if you plan on still having a relationship with them afterwards because once they say it and you hear it, they cannot take it back. Spare them by not listening.

Toxic people have a way of making you feel like everything is your fault. Whatever they did to you was because of something you supposedly did to them. They will not let you explain, they will yell, hit below the belt and talk over you. It is literally like talking to a brick wall. Do yourself a favor and let that shit go.

Self-care is everything. Exercise more, eat better, drink water, go to the doctor, go to the dentist, love yourself, and talk to a therapist. Do all the things that you need to survive. Do it on purpose, with purpose. Stop making excuses and get it done. Learn to take care of you first.

If 2020 has not taught us enough already, I want to challenge you from this point on to survive on purpose. Live your life to the fullest on purpose. Be your own boss on purpose. Be happy on purpose. Get your next promotion on purpose. Take time for yourself on purpose. Travel on purpose. Spend time with your family on purpose. Learn something new on purpose. Love on purpose. Conquer your fears on purpose. Take care of yourself on purpose. Whatever goals you have for yourself, complete them on purpose. Let us make 2021 the best year yet, on purpose.

CHAPTER ELEVEN
GOD'S PURPOSE FOR YOUR LIFE IS
BIGGER THAN YOU!

As I stated at the beginning of this book, writing a book was never, ever, ever, ever, ever in my plans. If God had not kept bringing me back to it and guiding me along the way, Mannnnn, I would have never thought twice about it. It gave me anxiety thinking about writing a book. That is why I ran from the idea for so long. I began to overthink everything. When I say everything, I mean everything.

My writing style how long does the book have to be, what am I going to talk about, do people really want to read what I have to say, and the list goes on. I remember when I started reading Michelle Obama's book, I said, "Man, I don't have 400 plus pages in me. I just don't."

That freaked me completely out. Then one day as I am strolling through Instagram, somebody posted this book called LEAP by Alexandria Norton. I brought the book.

As soon as I received the book, I checked to see how many pages there were. It was only sixty-three pages. I read the book right away. It was nobody but God that put that book in my timeline because I cannot for the life of me figure out who posted it but THANK YOU. LEAP was just what I needed to read for me to finish this book.

She talked about every fear that I had about writing a book. I realized that I was not the only one. God will give you all types of signs and help along the way to help you out and to remember your why. God had given me all the signs. I had to convince myself that my why is bigger than me. Now, that was a hard sell and still is. As afraid as I am of the outcome, I kept reminding myself that the Lord knows why He put this on my plate because it is bigger than me, and that keeps me going.

While attempting to finish my book, I got to the point where I was debating the words in my book. To curse or not to curse, was the question. When you read this book, I want you to feel like you are talking to me. If you know me, I love the Lord, but I curse a lot a bit. I was worried about what my readers would think about it. I am a work in progress. He ain't through with me yet. With my deadline rapidly approaching, I stopped writing for almost two months straight, and almost said to forget it completely.

One day I was listening to the radio or watching tv and someone was talking about the books that they had written. They went on to say that it was their fifth or so book. Their editor told them that that was their best book because it was about them, and he should have written it a long time ago if he had not let someone talk him out of doing so. Look at God! Won't He do it?! That was my sign. Thank goodness because I was very close to putting this book down again.

In writing this book, I realized that there is a thing called self-sabotage. Self-sabotage is when we actively or passively take steps to prevent ourselves from reaching our goals. This was ME. When I realized that is what I was doing, every time I thought about quitting that little voice would say, "Oh so you are just going to quit again?"

As much as I wanted to say, "Yes, got dammit!" I knew deep down that I did not want to quit again. I have quit so many things in my life because of self-sabotage. I am so over that. My why and my purpose is bigger than me.

To all my fellow self-sabotages, cut it out. We are better than that. We have so much to offer to the world. Shine as bright as the sun. Stop running from your passion and your purpose. The time will never be right and there will always be obstacles and hurdles for you to cross but you can do it, boo. You can have it all if you focus.

Let go of all that fear and make your dreams come true. I cannot wait to see what He has for us when we get out of our way. Remember, your why and your purpose is bigger than you. You must be intentional and purposeful to succeed at this thing called life.

If you find yourself taking two steps forward and ten steps backwards, think about what lesson God wants you to learn for you to get to the next level. God wants you to fully enjoy and appreciate what he has for you. So, dig deep, face your fears, and go for yours. You got this!

ACKNOWLEDGEMENTS

To My Lord and Savior, thank you for giving vision and guiding me every step of the way. Without you absolutely nothing would be possible. I am forever grateful. P.S. Thanks for putting me on in advance!

To my children, Aniyah & Karter, I must be the luckiest mom in the world to have kids as amazing as the two of you. I hope that mommy makes you proud with this book and shows you that you can do anything that you put your mind to. I love you two to the end of the earth and back like a million times.

To my husband, thank you for your love and support through all my wild ideas with this being the craziest. You are appreciated.

To My Mommy, thank you for EVERYTHING and paving the way for me to be great. You rock like no other.

To my Dad, thanks for being all that you have been to me.

To my GrandmaDot, thanks for all your love and support.

To my siblings, my hero and sheros, I swear y'all are the Greatest of All Time! I would not trade you guys for nothing in the world. I have learned so much from the three of you. I love and appreciate each of you more than you know.

To my nieces and nephews, I absolutely love being your Auntie Kan. I hope each of you are as proud of me as I am of you. I love y'all so much.

To my friends, thank you for all the love, support and encouraging words throughout this process. Love y'all, mean it.

To Everyone that reads this book, THANK YOU SOOO MUCH for your support, you literally could have been doing anything with your time, but you chose to read my book. I appreciate that for real! I hope it blesses your entire soul.

Khandilyn Hicks- Hairstylist IG @iconicshearz

Nikki Rountree- MUA IG @nikki_sadea

Skie Harris- face enhancement IG @skieartlounge

Ericka Moore- photographer IG

@erickamoorephotos

Thank you so much ladies for bringing my

vision to life for my cover!

ABOUT THE AUTHOR

Kandis (Riddick) Rainey was born on

September 23,1981 and was not envisioning a

future of motivating women when she

experienced what later became the foundation

for Purposefully Scarred. From a young age, Kandis knew that an individual's success in life was ultimately determined by personal choices and perceptions of situations. She learned early how to view a cup as half full and not half empty. It is this mindset that enabled her to overcome a devastating life event that would have destroyed others. As a young woman, she decided to use her experiences to motivate and guide the lives of other women. Kandis tapped into her passion by pursuing a career path as a Middle School/ High School Educator and Athletic Coach. For Kandis, this was an avenue to reach young women during the most impressionable stages of life. She assured that her messages about the importance of maintaining a vision for the future grabbed the attention of each of her students and players.

After years of motivation, at a small scale,

Kandis has opted to face her fears, listen to

God, and live in a real uncomfortable place.

Purposefully Scarred is an effort to share an

example of how experiences can shape you

rather than break you.